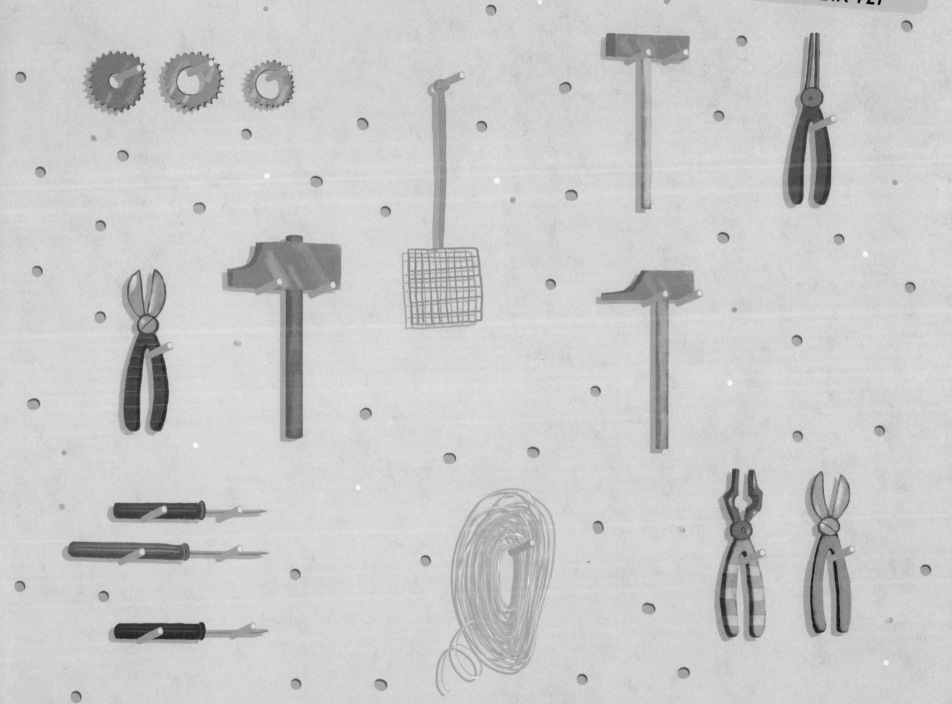

GOLDILOCKS AND THE THREE ENGINEERS

Sue Fliess   pictures by Petros Bouloubasis

Albert Whitman & Company
Chicago, Illinois

In a tiny bungalow,
there lived a clever thinker.
Young Goldilocks invented things.
She'd make and craft and tinker.

Gadgets that could zip your coat
and tie your tennis shoes.
Tools that help you seek and find
whatever you might lose.

But Goldilocks was in a rut.
She had inventor's block.
"I have no inspiration left.
I need to take a walk."

In the meantime, three smart bears all worked in preparation for one delicious feast before their winter hibernation.

"On that hill," said Papa Bear,
"The honey is the best."
"When we get there," Mama yawned,
"we'll eat and then we'll rest."

When they'd finished up their meal,
they spied a bungalow.
"We could spend the winter there.
It's sheltered from the snow!"

"No one's home," said Mama Bear,
and opened up the door.
The room was full of strange devices,
widgets, tools, and more!

"Look at this!" said Papa Bear.
"A chair made just for you!
It feeds you and it wipes your mouth,
and reads you stories, too!"

"Oh my goodness!" Mama said,
"A porridge-stirring bowl."
"And this bed rocks you right to sleep—
all with remote control!"

Baby Bear climbed in the chair.
"I wish it had some tires."
So Papa added four small wheels,
with nuts and bolts and pliers.

Mama put some porridge on.
"It's over-stirred and runny.
This concoction simply needs
a touch of golden honey."

"We can't just stay," said Papa Bear.
"It really isn't right."
"But now it's dark," said Baby Bear.
"So maybe just tonight?"

They crawled in bed and turned it on.
It rocked them all about.
But then it sped up, swung too fast,
and flipped the bears right out!

Baby fixed the engine block,
replaced the gears that burned.
Soon the bears were fast asleep...
Then Goldilocks returned.

"Who's been reading in my chair?
And now it rolls around!
I'll admit, this makes more sense
and covers lots of ground."

"Who's been eating porridge here?
It's creamier somehow...
Ooh, there's honey in the mix.
It tastes much better now!"

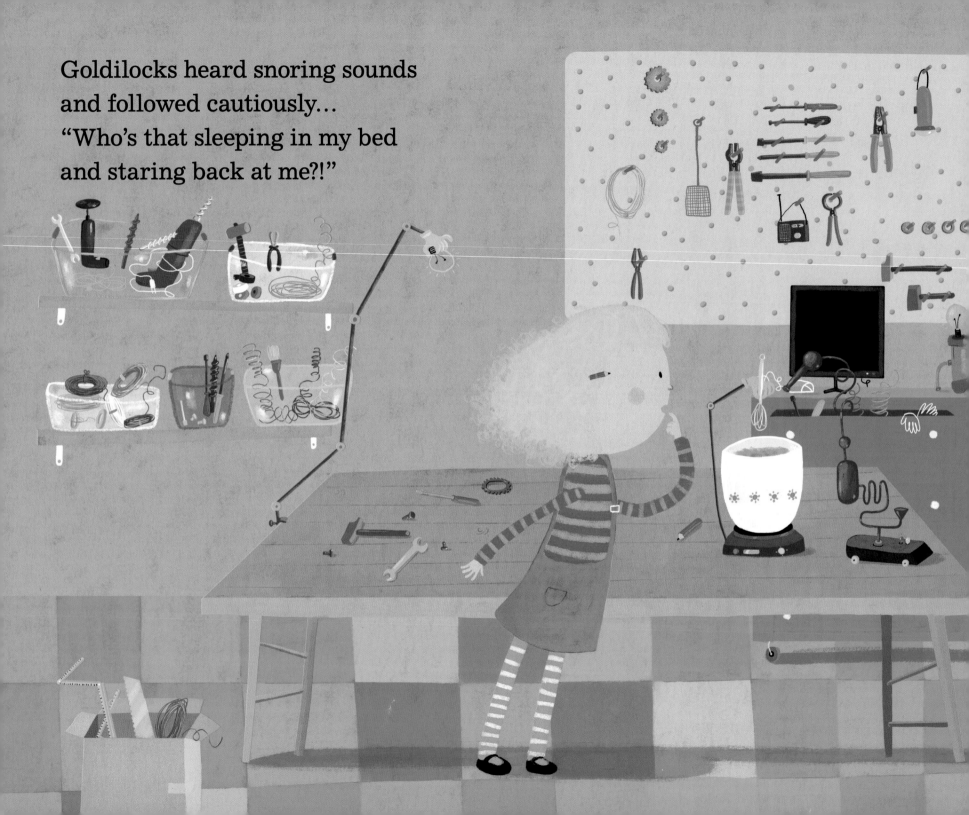

Goldilocks heard snoring sounds
and followed cautiously...
"Who's that sleeping in my bed
and staring back at me?!"

"Yikes!" the bears all cried at once.
"We know how this appears.
We truly couldn't help ourselves—
we're three bear engineers!"

The three bears then explained themselves.
"We hope you'll understand.
For as you know, experiments
don't always go as planned."

"You've improved my projects here,
and made them much more fun.
Proving that four brains, by far,
are better than just one!"

"Perhaps what I was looking for was not more inspiration, but engineers to team with me and bring their innovation."

Goldilocks and these three bears
exchanged ideas all night.
Their teamwork triumphed in the end
and things turned out just right.

Soon the three bears had to leave.
"We'll meet up in the spring."
"And when we do," said Goldilocks,
"We'll make the next big thing!"

For my brother-in-law, Mark, a very smart bear.—SF

To Dimitra—PB

Library of Congress Cataloging-in-Publication data is on file with the publisher.

Text copyright © 2021 by Sue Fliess
Illustrations copyright © 2021 by Albert Whitman & Company
Illustrations by Petros Bouloubasis
First published in the United States of America in 2021 by Albert Whitman & Company
ISBN 978-0-8075-2997-3 (hardcover)
ISBN 978-0-8075-3000-9 (ebook)

Printed in China
10 9 8 7 6 5 4 3 2 1 WKT 24 23 22 21 20

Design by Rick DeMonico

For more information about Albert Whitman & Company,
visit our website at www.albertwhitman.com.